*This one is for Lisa and Jonelle, because you were
there when my brows went really, really bad.
And you laughed. Nice.*
—J.C.E.

For Molly, Sam, and Luke
—M.P.

The illustrations in this book were made with
a combination of pencil, paper, and digital paint.

Cataloging-in-Publication Data has been applied for and may be obtained
from the Library of Congress.

ISBN 978-1-4197-2537-1

Text copyright © 2020 Jason Carter Eaton
Illustrations copyright © 2020 Mike Petrik
Book design by Steph Stilwell

Printed and bound in China
10 9 8 7 6 5 4 3 2 1

Abrams Books for Young Readers are available at special discounts when purchased
in quantity for premiums and promotions as well as fundraising or educational use.
Special editions can also be created to specification. For details, contact
specialsales@abramsbooks.com or the address below.

Abrams® is a registered trademark of Harry N. Abrams, Inc.

ABRAMS The Art of Books
195 Broadway, New York, NY 10007
abramsbooks.com

Abrams Books for Young Readers • New York

By **Jason Carter Eaton**   Illustrated by **Mike Petrik**

BAD
BROWS

Bernard . . .

never really . . .

gave much thought . . .

to his eyebrows.

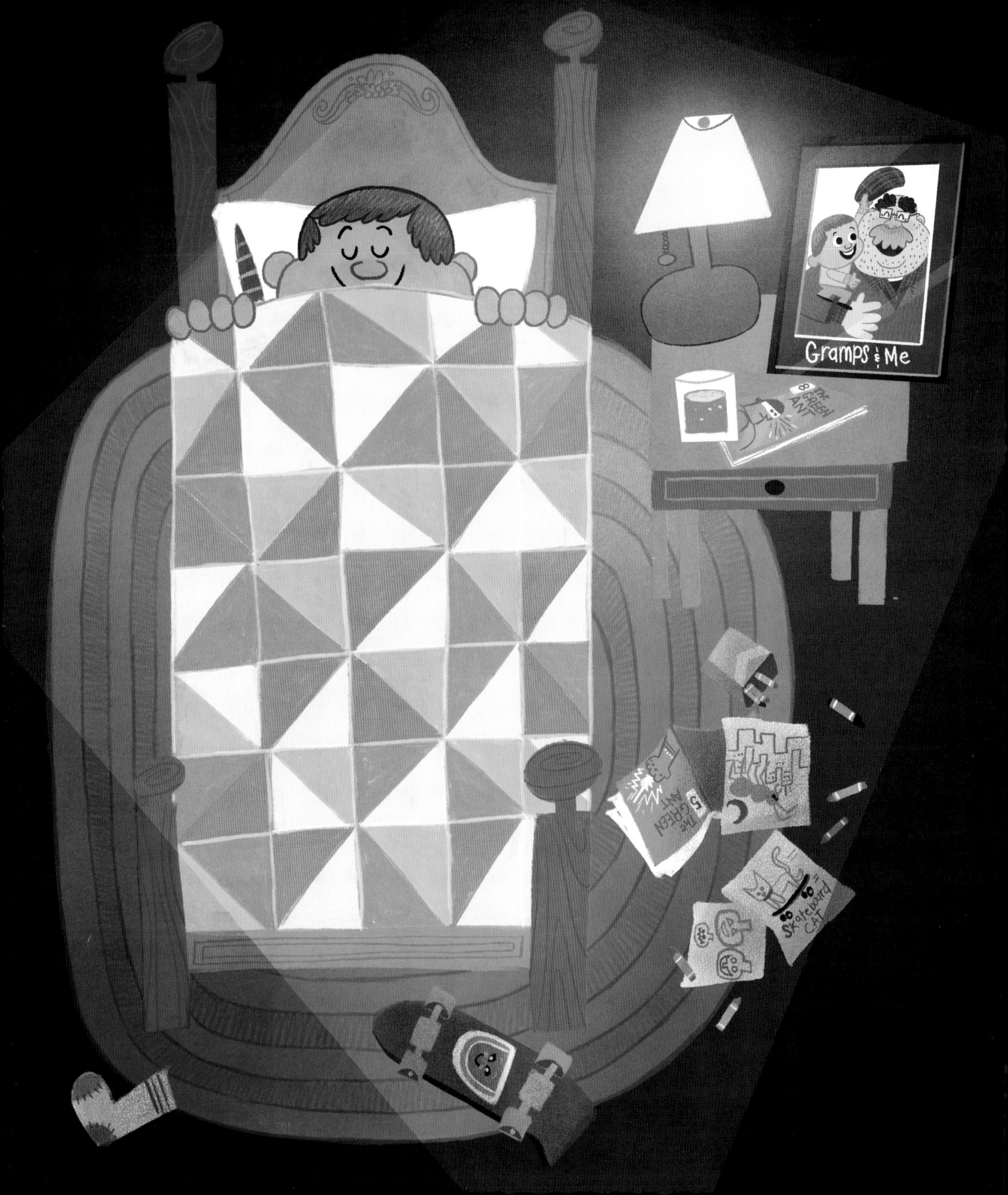

At first, he thought his eyebrows were just
a bit rumpled, so he smoothed them out.
But at breakfast . . .

"What's with the goofy face?" asked his dad.
"I dunno," said Bernard. "It's my eyebrows."

"Mom!" screamed his brother.
"Bernard's making funny faces at me!"
"You'd better not do that when Grandpa
wakes up," scolded his mom.
"I-bow," added his baby sister.

The bus ride to school was high-brow.

Class was low-brow.

And Picture Day was absolutely weird-brow.

All day long, Bernard's eyebrows worked hard to confound him.

He liked today's lunch . . .
but it didn't seem that way.

He found the math lesson easy
. . . but it sure didn't look like it.

Bernard was starting to panic.
But he appeared quite calm.

The principal tried to straighten Bernard out.
"Bernard, your eyebrows are your face's way of telling other people how you feel. They show when you're happy, sad, scared, excited, curious, or angry. Do you understand?"

Bernard nodded.
"Then why doesn't it look like you're taking
this seriously?" asked the principal.
"I wish I knew," said Bernard.
But he was sent home anyway.

Home was no better, though.
"Excuse me," scolded his mom.
"Are you scowling at the goldfish?"

"Not on purpose," groaned Bernard.

Perhaps his eyebrows just needed some grooming.
So his parents brought him to the barber.
"Those sure are some wild eyebrows you've got there, son.
Don't worry, we'll have them tamed in no time."

But the moment the barber approached
Bernard's brows, they went into hiding.

"Never mind,"
sighed Bernard.

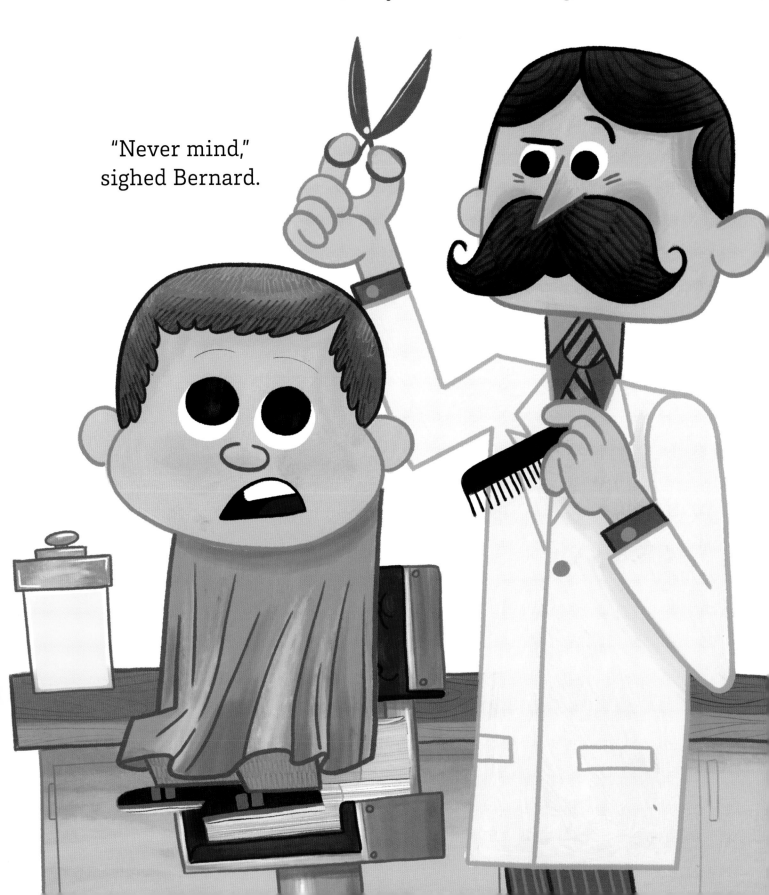

Perhaps his eyebrows were ill.
So Bernard's parents took him to
the doctor's office.

But when he left, they were worse.
Far worse.

Bernard's brows weren't just bad anymore—

they were dangerous . . .

and dastardly . . .

and downright disgusting.

Bernard was absolutely miserable.
It seemed as though he was doomed
to a life with bad brows.

Until there was a
knock at the door . . .

It was his *real* eyebrows—he'd recognize them anywhere!

Those bad ones must have been *imposters*!

Bernard was himself again.
Even though he never really learned
why his eyebrows went on vacation
(because eyebrows can't talk—that would be silly),
Bernard was thrilled to have them back.

And he would never take his
eyebrows for granted again.

"I know I never really thought about you before,
brows," said Bernard, "but from now on,
you'll always be on my mind."

And they were.

Bernard and his eyebrows enjoyed making many exciting expressions that night. And as he climbed into bed, Bernard lovingly smoothed out his brows and drifted off to sleep, reflecting on what a long, strange day it had been.

"Wait," said Bernard, waking up with a start.
"If these are *my* eyebrows ... then ...
whose bad brows were on my face?

And more importantly ..."